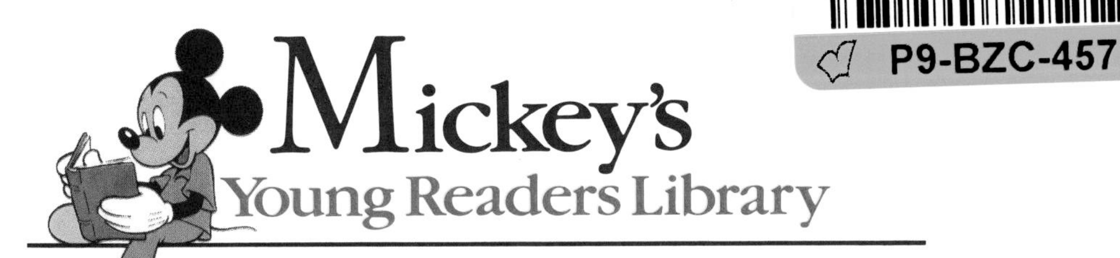

VOLUME
15

Goofy Goes to the Fair

STORY BY MARY PACKARD

Activities by Thoburn Educational Enterprises, Inc.

A BANTAM BOOK
NEW YORK · TORONTO · LONDON · SYDNEY · AUCKLAND

ISBN 0–553–05630–1

Published simultaneously in the United States and Canada. Bantam Books are published by Bantam Doubleday Dell Publishing Group, Inc. Its trademark, consisting of the words "Bantam Books" and the portrayal of a rooster, is Registered in U.S. Patent and Trademark Office and in other countries. Marca Registrada. Bantam Books 666 Fifth Avenue, New York, New York 10103.
Printed in the United States of America
0 9 8 7 6 5 4 3 2 1

A Walt Disney BOOK FOR YOUNG READERS

It was the first day of the County Fair. Nobody wanted to miss it. Especially not Goofy. He whistled a happy tune as he climbed into his car, *Old Faithful.* It took him a few tries to start up the engine. But soon he was on his way. He thought about the rides and games. He thought about the cotton candy. He didn't see the steam that was coming from the front of the car.

GOOFY

Mickey was on his way to the fair, too.

"The fast new express train is the best way to go," thought Mickey. "I'll get my ticket at the station."

But when Mickey got to the station, he heard some bad news.

"I'm sorry, sir," said the clerk. "Our trains don't go anywhere near the fair. Maybe you should try the bus instead." Then he handed Mickey a bus schedule.

Mickey looked at the schedule. He looked at his watch. "Oh, no," he exclaimed. "The bus leaves in ten minutes."

He raced toward the bus stop. But before Mickey could reach it, the bus pulled away. Just then, Goofy drove up beside Mickey.

"Hey, Mickey," he called. "*Old Faithful* and I are on our way to the fair. Would you like a ride?"

"Thanks," panted Mickey, "but the road to the fair is pretty rough. There's a big mountain to get over, too. It looks like *Old Faithful* is already having trouble, Goofy." Mickey stared at the steaming car.

"Oh, that's just *Old Faithful's* radiator acting up again," said Goofy. "All it needs is a drink of water, and we'll be ready to go!"

Goofy got out of the car. "Splash, splash, splash," went the water as he poured it into the thirsty car.

"See?" said Goofy. "Good as new."

"Are you sure we can make it?" asked Mickey.

"I think we can," answered Goofy.

"Well, then," Mickey declared, "Let's get going. There's no time to lose."

Minnie and Daisy had arrived at the bus stop in time to take the bus to the fair. Each of them hoped to win a ribbon. As they happily rode along on the big new bus, Minnie showed Daisy the quilt she had made for the crafts contest. Daisy showed Minnie the pie she was planning to enter in the pie-baking contest.

"That pie smells great!" declared Minnie. "You'll win a blue ribbon for sure! If we get to the fair in time, that is!"

"This bus won't have any trouble getting to the fair in time," Daisy said.

But the big new bus was very big. Soon it came to a very low bridge.

"This bus will not fit under that bridge," the driver said sadly. "I guess we won't be going to the fair after all!"

"What will we do?" asked Minnie.

Daisy looked sad. "It looks like there's one thing we won't be doing," she replied. "We won't be winning any blue ribbons!"

Meanwhile, Goofy's car chugged along.

"Clank, clank," went the doors. "Squeak, squeak," went the wheels. "Rattle, rattle," went the engine.

"Gawrsh, it looks like that bus can't fit under the bridge," said Goofy. "And there's Minnie and Daisy. They must be on their way to the fair." Goofy slammed on the brakes. "Need a ride?" he asked.

Minnie and Daisy looked at Goofy's little old car. Then they looked back at the big new bus.

"Do you really think we'll make it all the way to the fair?" Daisy asked.

"I think we can," Goofy told her. So Minnie and Daisy got in the car, and off they all went.

Huey, Dewey, and Louie were singing in the back of Farmer Stillwagon's truck. They were happy to be on their way to the fair.

Just then, they came to a sharp turn. Farmer Stillwagon turned the wheel as hard as he could. But he didn't notice a family of raccoons just around the bend.

"Watch out!" cried Dewey in alarm.

"Hold on!" shouted Farmer Stillwagon.

"Yikes!" cried the boys, as the truck rolled off the road.

Then everyone got out to push. They pushed and pushed and pushed some more. But they could not push the truck back onto the road.

"I'll have to go home for help," said the farmer. "Maybe you boys can try walking to the fair." Then he turned to go.

"I guess we'll have to wait until next year to ride the giant roller coaster," sighed Louie.

The unhappy little boys did their best to cheer each other up. Then suddenly, they heard a noise.

"Clank, clank, squeak, squeak, screech, screech, SCREECH!"

"What is that?" asked Huey.

Just then Goofy's car came around the bend. Wheels squeaking, tires squealing, engine rattling, *Old Faithful* chugged along.

"Hooray!" the boys cried.

"Need a ride to the fair?" asked Goofy.

"Do we ever!" exclaimed Dewey, "But are you sure *Old Faithful* will make it?" Dewey asked.

"We think it will!" everyone said.

Then Goofy pulled an oil can from the trunk. "Glug, glug, glug," went the oil as Goofy poured. Soon the car was on its way.

Donald looked down at the road below. He was floating high in the sky in a hot-air balloon. That was how he was going to the fair.

"Hello," he called to his friends. Then he said to himself, "I guess Goofy and the gang are on their way to the fair, too. But I can't believe they think *Old Faithful* will get them there! It's such a long way, and the road is so hilly and bumpy."

All of a sudden there was a big puff of wind.
Donald's balloon zoomed past the noisy old car.
"So long," he shouted.

Soon Donald spotted the top of the Ferris wheel. "I've made it!" he cried happily.

But at the very last minute, the wind suddenly changed. Instead of blowing Donald's balloon toward the fair, it was blowing him away!

"Hey," yelled Donald. "I'm going the wrong way!"

Now Donald could not see the Ferris wheel anymore. But that was not all. The balloon was floating lower and lower. "Bumpety, bump, bump, bump," went the balloon. Before he knew it, Donald was on the ground.

"This is just great!" Donald sputtered. "Now what am I going to do?"

At that moment, Donald heard a familiar "beep, beep!" It was Goofy to the rescue! All of a sudden Goofy's old car didn't look so bad. In fact, it looked downright wonderful.

"Am I glad to see you!" cried Donald. "Have you got room for one more?"

"Sure, climb in," replied Goofy.

Just then, *Old Faithful* hit a great big hole in the road. "Hissssssss," went the air from the tire.

"Oh, no," Donald groaned. "I knew we weren't going to make it!"

"Of course we will," said Goofy. "*Old Faithful* just needs a little help." So Goofy and his friends helped change *Old Faithful's* tire. In no time at all, they were on their way.

"Wow, this road is so steep that I can't even see the top!" exclaimed Huey, as the little car climbed slowly up the mountain.

"The top does look very high," agreed Mickey.

"Maybe we should just turn around," suggested Daisy.

"We'll never make it!" groaned Huey.

"I knew this road was too hard for this car," moaned Donald.

Goofy looked all the way up at the top of the mountain. He patted the car. "Let's just give it a try," Goofy said.

The faithful old car huffed and puffed. Then it leaped forward with one great big jump. "Here we go!" Goofy shouted. Sure enough, the tired old car crept up, up, and up the mountain, until it was nearly at the top. Then it gave a great shiver and a loud sigh. Slowly, it began to roll back down the road.

"Come on, old friend! You can do it!"

The car wheezed. The car coughed. Then it began to move.

Up, up, up it crawled. They all sat on the edges of their seats.

"I think we can do it," said Goofy.

"I think we can, too," repeated Mickey, crossing his fingers.

Before long, everyone in the car was shouting, "I think we can! I think we can! I think we can!"

The faithful old car did its very best. It huffed and it puffed, and it chugged its way up. Until . . . it was almost there! *Old Faithful* had just a few yards to go. But, with a sputter and a mighty cough, it stopped in its tracks!

"We can't give up now!" cried Mickey, jumping out to push.

The others joined him. Goofy steered. They pushed and pushed until they were all out of breath.

"Just a little bit more to go!" gasped Donald.

"Let's all give one big push together!" called Mickey.

"We think we can, we think we can," the friends chanted.

And with a one, two, three, PUSH! the faithful old car coughed and . . . started!

"Hooray!" they all shouted. They jumped in just as *Old Faithful* rounded the top of the hill. And the faithful old car sailed down the mountain lickety-split.

"Clank, clank, clank!" went the doors. "Squeak, squeak, squeak!" went the wheels. "Rattle, rattle, rattle!" went the engine.

But no one was listening. They were too busy cheering.

"We knew we could! We knew we could! We knew we could!" they cried. Goofy, *Old Faithful*, and all of their friends had made it to the fair at last!

Think About It

Who Went To The Fair?

Do you remember who went to the fair and how they were planning to get there? If you need help remembering, look back at the story.

After your child does the activities in this book, refer to the *Young Readers Guide* for the answers to these activities and for additional games, activities, and ideas.

Getting To The Fair

After you've read the story, see how many of the details you remember. Tell whether or not each sentence is true or false.

True or False?

1. At first, Mickey thought *Old Faithful* was a great way to get to the fair.
2. Before they got into Goofy's car, Daisy and Minnie weren't so sure that *Old Faithful* would make it to the fair.
3. Huey, Dewey, and Louie were very happy to see *Old Faithful* drive up beside them.
4. When Donald was flying high in his balloon in the sky, he wished that he could be riding in *Old Faithful* with the rest of his friends.
5. Goofy knew that if he and his friends believed in *Old Faithful,* and if they all tried hard enough, they would make it to the fair.

Fun With Words

What Sound Does It Make?

Look at the sound words.

beep screech

cough rattle

Do you remember:
What sound the horn on *Old Faithful* makes?
What sound the doors make?
What sound the brakes make?
What sounds did *Old Faithful* make on its way to the top of the hill?

What's At The Fair?

Read each word. Find the picture of the thing it names. Name some other things in the picture.

pie
quilt
roller coaster
merry-go-round
Ferris wheel

ickey's
ickey's Young Readers Library • Mickey's Young Readers Library • Mickey's Youn
oung Readers Library • Mickey's Young Readers Library • Mickey's Young Reader
ickey's Young Readers Library • Mickey'